LiVING iN THE ARCTiC

Patty Whitehouse

Rourke

Publishing LLC

Vero Beach, Florida 32964

© 2007 Rourke Publishing LLC

www.rourkepublishing.com

PHOTO CREDITS: © Lynn M. Stone: title page, pages, 5, 8, 9, 11, 14, 18, 21; © Silense: pages 4, 19; © Jussi Santa Niemi: page 7; © Anette Linnea: page 10; © PhotoDisc: page 12; © Gordon Laurens: page 13; © Joe Gough: page 15; © Sandra Minarik: page 16; © Corel: pages 17, 20; ˙Steffen Foerster: page 22.

Editor: Robert Stengard-Olliges

Cover and interior design by Nicola Stratford

Library of Congress Cataloging-in-Publication Data

Whitehouse, Patricia, 1958-
  Living in the Arctic / Patty Whitehouse.
     p. cm. -- (Animal habitats)
  Includes index.
  ISBN 1-60044-188-2 (hard cover)
  ISBN 1-59515-546-5 (soft cover)
  1. Ecology--Arctic regions--Juvenile literature. 2. Arctic regions--Juvenile literature. I. Title. II. Series: Whitehouse, Patricia, 1958- Animal habitats.
  QH84.1.W48 2007
  578.0911'3--dc22

2006017640

Printed in the USA

CG/CG

Rourke Publishing

www.rourkepublishing.com – sales@rourkepublishing.com
Post Office Box 3328, Vero Beach, FL 32964

TABLE OF CONTENTS

WHAT IS THE ARCTIC?

The arctic is near the North Pole. Arctic summers are cool and short. Winters are very long.

The sun does not go down on some summer days.

The sun does not come up on some winter days.

HOW ARE ARCTIC PLANTS DIFFERENT?

Tall trees cannot grow in the arctic. Other arctic plants are small. Most arctic plants have small leaves and short roots. They help the plant grow quickly.

MOSS AND LICHEN

Moss is a tiny plant. It grows on rocks and on the ground in the arctic.

Lichens grow on rocks, too. Lichen is not a plant. It is two living things that work together to grow.

FLOWERS AND BERRIES

Arctic plants have tiny flowers. Flowers **bloom** for a short time in the arctic.

Some arctic plants grow fruit. Berries grow on **shrubs** in the summer.

HOW ARE ARCTIC ANIMALS DIFFERENT?

Arctic animals need to stay warm. Many have a lot of fat under their skin. This fat is called **blubber**.

Some animals turn white in winter. Then they can hide in the snow. Other animals sleep when it gets cold.

TUNNELERS AND FLIERS

Arctic hares are small and furry. They make tunnels in the snow during the winter months.

Puffins live near the oceans. They eat fish. Puffins can carry many fish in its beak at a time.

UNDER THE WATER

Beluga whales live in cold ocean water. They are the only whale that is white.

Seals spend most of their time in the water. Seal **pups** are good swimmers.

ANTLERS AND FUR

Caribou have big **antlers**. The antlers break off in fall.
They grow back in spring.

Polar bears have thick fur to help them keep warm.
Their fur looks white. But it is really **transparent**.

CAN PEOPLE LIVE IN THE ARCTIC?

People have lived in the arctic for a long time. They learned to hunt, fish, and keep warm.

People still use dog **sleds** to move on the snow. They use kayaks to move in the water.

LEAVING THE COLD

Some animals leave the arctic when it gets cold. The arctic tern flies to the South Pole each year.

Glossary

antlers (ANT lurz) — horns that fall off every year

bloom (BLOOM) — grow flowers

blubber (BLUH bur) — layer of fat that keeps animals warm

pups (PUHPS) — baby seals

sled (SLED) — a vehicle used to travel over snow

shrub (SHRUB) — plant smaller than a tree

transparent (transs PAIR uhnt) — clear or see-through

Index

FURTHER READING

Glassman, Jackie. *Amazing Arctic Animals*. Grosset and Dunla, 2002.
Hiscock, Bruce. *The Big Caribou Herd: Life in the Arctic National Wildlife Refuge*. Boyds Mills Press, 2003.
Miller, Debbie S. *Arctic Lights, Arctic Nights*. Walker Books, 2003.

WEBSITES TO VISIT

www.mbgnet.net
www.enchantedlearning.com/coloring/arcticanimals.shtml
www.saskschools.ca/~gregory/arctic/Awildlife.html

ABOUT THE AUTHOR

Patty Whitehouse has been a teacher for 17 years. She is currently a Lead Science teacher in Chicago, where she lives with her husband and two teenage children. She is the author of more than 100 books about science for children.